BIG APPLE BARN™

ROSCOE AND THE PONY PARADE

WELCOME TO
BIG APPLE BARN!

ROSCOE AND THE
PONY PARADE

by **KRISTIN EARHART**

**Illustrations by
JOHN STEVEN GURNEY**

SCHOLASTIC INC.
New York Toronto London Auckland Sydney
Mexico City New Delhi Hong Kong Buenos Aires

*To Shannon Penney, who is as steadfast as Big Ben, as
sweet as Goldilocks, as understanding as Gracie, as wise
as Prudence, as clever as Roscoe, and as loyal as Happy.*
—*K.J.E.*

No part of this publication may be reproduced, stored in a retrieval system,
or transmitted in any form or by any means, electronic, mechanical,
photocopying, recording, or otherwise, without written permission of
the publisher. For information regarding permission, write to Scholastic Inc.,
Attention: Permissions Department, 557 Broadway, New York, NY 10012.

ISBN-13: 978-0-545-03472-2
ISBN-10: 0-545-03472-8

Text copyright © 2008 by Kristin Earhart.
Illustrations copyright © 2008 by Scholastic Inc.
SCHOLASTIC, LITTLE APPLE, BIG APPLE BARN, and associated logos are
trademarks and/or registered trademarks of Scholastic Inc.

12 11 10 9 8 7 6 5 4 3 2   8 9 10 11 12 13/0
                                            40

Printed in the U.S.A.
First printing, January 2008

Contents

Chapter One

Sassy Speaks Up

"Can you smell that?" Sassy asked, her mane fluttering in the breeze. "It smells like spring."

Happy lifted his nose in the air and drew in a deep breath, savoring the sweetness. He knew the scent well. "It's honeysuckle. There's a bush over there, on the other side of the fence," Happy said, swishing his shiny black tail toward the far corner of the pasture. He had been watching the bush all spring, waiting to spot some yellow-and-white buds. "It just bloomed this weekend. It's beautiful!"

Sassy, a young appaloosa pony, glanced toward the other end of the field. "Well, while you were here watching the flowers, I was off winning blue ribbons for Big Apple Barn," Sassy teased.

Happy knew that his friend had just returned from a show. She had talked about it a lot before the big weekend, and she had practiced hard. Sassy and her rider, Andrea, were very serious about shows. "Congratulations, Sassy. Andrea must be proud of you."

"She is." Sassy confirmed with a nod. "We jumped like the wind and whizzed around the courses. Andrea gave me bunches of carrots when we were finished."

The word *carrots* made Happy's mouth water. He didn't get very excited about shows, but he did like getting special treats. Really, didn't all ponies love carrots? And apples? And clover? Happy loved honeysuckle, too. The flowers only bloomed for a short time, and the petals were very small. But Happy liked how they tickled his tongue. They were like the first taste of spring.

"Hey, Happy! Hey, Sassy!" a tiny gray mouse called. He was out of breath from climbing a nearby fence post. Now he stood on top of it, waving his front paws in the air to get the ponies' attention.

"Hello, Roscoe," Happy said, heading over to the mouse. Sassy followed close behind. "It's good to see you."

The word *carrots* made Happy's mouth water. He didn't get very excited about shows, but he did like getting special treats. Really, didn't all ponies love carrots? And apples? And clover? Happy loved honeysuckle, too. The flowers only bloomed for a short time, and the petals were very small. But Happy liked how they tickled his tongue. They were like the first taste of spring.

"Hey, Happy! Hey, Sassy!" a tiny gray mouse called. He was out of breath from climbing a nearby fence post. Now he stood on top of it, waving his front paws in the air to get the ponies' attention.

"Hello, Roscoe," Happy said, heading over to the mouse. Sassy followed close behind. "It's good to see you."

"Roscoe, you did notice that we're fenced in, didn't you?" Sassy asked. "Ponies can't just stroll into the woods whenever they want."

"So? We can still walk in the field," Roscoe insisted as Happy set off at an easy pace. "I just love spring." The mouse spread his paws wide and looked up at the clear blue sky.

"Well, if you love spring, then you should go to the Spring Fling in town," Sassy said, hurrying to catch up with Happy and Roscoe. "Andrea said it's a big festival with a parade. Plus, there are games and rides. Doesn't that sound like fun? It's next weekend."

Just then, Andrea appeared at the gate. "Sassy," she called. "Time for our lesson."

Sassy's ears pricked forward. "Well, I guess I'll have to join you another day. Have a good walk." Happy and Roscoe watched her spotted hindquarters as she trotted away.

"She's got a lot of nerve," Roscoe huffed. "Who is she to say what we should do if we love spring? I would much rather walk with you than go into town for a festival."

Happy looked up toward his ears, where his friend was perched. He could not see Roscoe, but Happy guessed that the mouse had a scowl on his face.

"What's so springy about a festival?" Roscoe went on.

"Well," Happy said, "I'm not sure."

"Sassy always makes a big deal out of everything," Roscoe complained. "If it's not a show, it's a silly festival. Who cares about a parade?"

Happy kept his eyes on the honeysuckle bush. He enjoyed the simple pleasures of spring as much as anyone, like walking around the pasture with Roscoe. It was the perfect way to spend an afternoon. But he decided not to answer the mouse's last question. Happy didn't know much about parades, but he thought the festival sounded like good pony fun.

Chapter Two

A Festive Family

Happy looked out over his stall door, waiting patiently. It had been three days since he had seen his favorite rider, Ivy Marshall. That was just too long!

Ivy was Andrea's little sister. Their mother was Diane, the trainer at Big Apple Barn. She taught kids how to ride ponies and horses. Happy and Sassy were both lesson ponies.

Happy liked all of his riders, but he liked Ivy the most. He and Ivy made the perfect team. Ivy liked to take lessons and jump fences, but she also loved long trail rides and brushing Happy in his stall. There were times when Happy believed Ivy could read his mind. She could actually think like a pony!

Happy whinnied as Ivy came around the corner with her mom and Andrea.

"Happy! Guess what?" Ivy cried, springing toward the pony's stall.

"Ivy, no running in the barn," Diane warned. "You know it might scare the horses."

Ivy skidded to a stop, then walked quickly toward Happy. When she reached his stall, she bounced up and down. "We're riding in the parade at the Spring Fling. We're riding in the parade!"

Happy pricked his ears forward. *The parade?*

As Ivy opened Happy's stall door and led him into the aisle, she told him more. "We're all going. My whole family, and you, Sassy, Big Ben, and Goldi."

Happy nodded his head up and down. He had been excited when Ivy first said they were going to the parade, but it would be even better with Sassy, Big Ben, and Goldi there. Big Ben was Diane's own show horse, a tall, chestnut jumper. Goldi was a short, slightly plump lesson pony with a caramel-colored coat and a long blond mane and tail. They were both Happy's friends. They always gave him good advice.

"We usually go *to* the parade, but I've never been *in* the parade," Ivy explained. "It'll be so much fun!" Ivy threw her arms around Happy's neck, and Happy sighed, glad to have her nearby.

"Ivy, it's time for your lesson," Andrea

said, tapping her watch. "Are you going to ride Happy or are you going to hug him all day?"

Ivy blushed. "Andrea thinks she's so cool," she whispered to Happy. "But I know she's excited about the parade, too."

Happy could tell Ivy was excited because she did not pay attention during their lesson. First, she forgot to ask him to trot, then she forgot to ask him to stop. She did not point him at the correct part of the fence when it was time to jump.

Out of the corner of his eye, Happy could see the other lesson ponies watching them. He thought he noticed Goldi shaking her head.

After the lesson was over, Ivy led Happy over to Goldi. The older pony looked worried. "Happy, is everything okay? Ivy is always

such a good rider. What's wrong with her today?"

"Oh, she just can't concentrate. We found out we're going to the Spring Fling," Happy explained. "You're going, too!"

"My goodness!" Goldi exclaimed. "I haven't been to the Spring Fling in years." She seemed to be staring right past Happy as she spoke, her golden mane falling into her eyes.

"Really? You've been there before? What's it like?" Happy asked.

Goldi turned back to Happy. "It's like a circus, with games, rides, people, and animals everywhere." Suddenly, she looked very serious. "Mark my word, it's a circus. You'll need to keep your wits about you."

"I see," Happy replied. He wasn't sure how to react to Goldi's warning. "Well, is it fun?" he asked.

"Oh, yes," Goldi said. "There's a silly costume contest for the mascot of the parade, and there is good food everywhere. It's fun all right. But it can also get a little out of control."

Happy nodded. He had been to a horse show the previous year, and it was the same way. There was so much going on, it was hard to concentrate.

Happy looked at Goldi. Something about

the caramel-colored pony had changed. She was usually very calm and good-natured, which was why she was the pony that most beginners rode in lessons. But now she seemed . . . different. She held her head and tail up high. Her step had a bounce to it. "We're going to the Spring Fling," Happy heard her sing to herself as she walked away.

Seeing Goldi, Happy started to feel giddy. The festival was something brand-new — something he had never done before. He could hardly wait! But there was one big problem. He was afraid to tell Roscoe he was going. Happy had a feeling that his best buddy would not share his enthusiasm.

Chapter Three

On the Road

"Happy, I'm disappointed in you," Roscoe scolded. "You love Big Apple Barn as much as I do. So why did you let Sassy talk you into going to some silly parade? We could have had fun here today."

Happy looked at Roscoe and sighed. The mouse would not let it rest. He had been hounding Happy all week! Now it was the morning of the parade, and Roscoe still thought he could talk Happy out of going.

"Roscoe, we can have fun any day, but the Spring Fling is only today," Happy explained. "And Sassy didn't talk me into it. I *want* to go. I want to march in the parade with Ivy. It'll be fun to be there with Goldi and Big Ben, too. I don't get to see them that much anymore."

Roscoe's shoulders slumped. "Fine. I'll just stay here and chew wires by myself."

"What? What did you say?" Happy was shocked.

"Chew wires," Roscoe repeated. "I do it all the time. It's normal. Mice have to chew things to keep their teeth from growing too long." He rolled his eyes at Happy. "So I'll start by chewing some wire, then I'll raid the grain bin. I'd bring you some grain, but you won't be here."

Roscoe gave Happy a long look, but the

pony just shook his head. A few pieces of corn wouldn't change his mind.

"Then," Roscoe continued, "I'll take a nap in the tall grass out back. It's perfect this time of year. The spring sun is warm on your belly, but the grass is still nice and cool." The mouse closed his eyes and a smile stretched across his face. As Happy watched, he saw Roscoe peek at him and then pretend that he hadn't opened his eyes.

"It sounds like a good day," Happy said, tilting his head to the side and trying not to laugh.

"Yep," replied Roscoe. "That's all the excitement I need. I don't have to go searching for thrills. I can find them right here in my backyard."

"That's wonderful, Roscoe," Happy said. He reached down to nibble at a few remaining strands of hay on his stall floor. "You have a full day planned. You won't miss me at all."

Now that Happy had his head down, Roscoe could stare him right in the eye. "You're right. I won't miss you," Roscoe declared. Then he strode right under the door and out of the stall.

"You know he's just giving you a hard time, right?"

Happy looked up and saw Prudence, the barn cat, looking at him.

"He doesn't want you to go without him," Prudence explained. Her nose twitched, and she rubbed it with her paw. When she was done, her gaze returned to Happy. "Roscoe hates being left out."

"Well, he has a funny way of showing it," Happy replied.

"Does he?" Prudence asked, but she did not wait for a response. Her nose twitched again, and she walked away.

Happy sighed. He wasn't sure what Prudence had meant. The tabby cat often spoke in riddles. But Happy wouldn't have to think about it for long. Ivy would be there any minute, and then their adventure would begin.

Happy whinnied the second he heard the big barn door roll open. After a moment, Ivy and Andrea came around the corner. Happy heard Sassy whinny, too.

Ivy's arms swung back and forth as she approached Happy. The pony pawed at the stall floor. He wished she would hurry!

"Hello, boy," Ivy greeted him with a smile. "Today's the big day!" She rubbed the palm of her hand against his muzzle. Happy gave a playful snort.

Ivy quickly ran a brush over Happy's back. Then she brought him out in the aisle so she could put on his trailer wraps. Happy stamped his hooves as Ivy pulled the wraps around his legs. "Happy, stop that. I know you're excited, but please hold still! These wraps will keep you from hurting yourself on our trip," said Ivy. She ran her hand down his leg to try to soothe him, but Happy couldn't help stamping again. After a week of waiting and talking with Roscoe about the festival, he really wanted to go!

He watched Andrea lead Sassy down the aisle. Then the girls' dad stepped out of Goldi's stall, and the small pony followed behind him. Seeing Happy, Goldi lifted her nose and gave a friendly neigh. Happy looked back at Ivy, who was still busy working on his back wraps. *What's taking her so long?* he wondered. When Big Ben walked out of his stall with Diane, Happy could hardly contain his excitement. It was time! As soon as Ivy tightened his last leg wrap, the group would be off.

"That's it, Happy," Ivy finally said. "Your saddle and bridle are already in the trailer, so let's go." Ivy clicked her tongue, and Happy rushed down the barn aisle. "Okay, okay!" Ivy laughed, hanging on to the end of Happy's lead line. "Let me catch up!" She jogged next to the pony, her braids bouncing up and down on either side of her head.

Happy and Ivy arrived outside just in time to see Big Ben's chestnut tail disappear inside the trailer, which was hitched to

Diane's red pickup truck. There was a ramp leading up to the door. Happy nickered under his breath, feeling a bit nervous. He had never been in the big trailer before. It could hold six horses at a time! He was used to smaller, two-horse trailers.

"Come on, Happy," Ivy said, smiling at him. "What's the holdup?"

Happy took another long look. The trailer was new, and it was a little scary. But it wasn't so new or scary that he wouldn't get on. Nothing would keep him from enjoying this parade!

Happy took a deep breath, walked up the ramp, and backed into a skinny stall inside the trailer. Sassy was next to him, and Big Ben and Goldi were across from them.

"See you soon, Happy!" Ivy said, tying his lead line to the trailer stall. "Bye, everyone!"

Ivy waved, and Happy watched her boots as she went down the ramp.

Diane lifted the ramp and secured the door. There was a window on either side of the trailer, and golden sunshine streamed in from a skylight over Happy's head.

"It's a perfect day for a parade," Goldi said, looking up at the cloudless sky.

"It's lovely," Big Ben agreed.

Happy could hear the sweet chirping of birds. Spring was in the air! His stomach fluttered. The festival was only a short ride away.

Then the truck engine growled, and the tires began to crunch along the stone driveway.

"Wheeeee!"

Happy looked around. What was that? Happy pricked his ears forward and tried to hear better, but the voice was drowned out by the sound of Diane's truck.

"Brace yourself," Big Ben advised. "Diane is changing gears." All at once, the trailer lurched forward as the truck pulled onto the open road. Happy spread his hooves apart, so he could keep his balance. Then he heard the tiny voice again.

"Wooo-weee!"

Happy glanced at Big Ben and the other ponies. None of them had said anything. He followed the voice up, up, up.

"Uh-uh-uh-oooooooh!"

At that very moment, Happy saw something fall from the skylight. It was Roscoe! And he was tumbling down, down, down.

Chapter Four

Curiosity Caught the Mouse

Ker-plop!

The little mouse flipped twice in the air before hitting the trailer floor with a thud.

"Roscoe!" Happy cried in surprise. "What are you doing here?"

Sassy, Big Ben, and Goldi all stared at Happy. Goldi looked upset by Happy's lack of concern. Then Big Ben and the other ponies turned their attention back to Roscoe, who was still lying on the trailer floor. He was flat on his tummy, with his arms and legs spread out. His tail pointed straight up at the very skylight that he had fallen through.

"My, my, my," Goldi said in a soothing voice. "That was quite a fall. Are you all right?"

"What happened?" Roscoe asked, his voice muffled.

"You fell from the roof of the trailer," Big Ben explained.

"I did?" Roscoe questioned. He rolled over and rubbed his head. He blinked his eyes three times. "I'm seeing spots. Everything is fuzzy. My head is pounding."

"It'll get better," Big Ben said. "You just got the wind knocked out of you."

Meanwhile, Happy wondered if the mouse had had the sense knocked out of him, too. What had he been doing on top of the trailer? Roscoe had said he wanted to spend a quiet day at home, enjoying the simple pleasures of spring. Now he was headed for the hubbub of town — the excitement of the festival *and* the parade.

Goldi nuzzled the mouse's belly, which made Roscoe giggle. "That tickles," he said, playfully pushing the pony's nose away with his paw.

"Awww. You'll be feeling better in no time," Goldi assured him.

"I hope so," said the mouse. He stood up and brushed himself off, then smoothed the hair on the tips of his ears. "Well, since I'm here, I might as well go to town with you." He glanced over at Happy and bit his lip.

Happy rolled his eyes. He suspected that Roscoe had been on top of the trailer on purpose. His big-eared buddy must have wanted an excuse to go to the parade, just like Prudence had said!

"I've never been to town before," Roscoe went on. "Is it a lot different from life at the barn?"

"Just sit back, and you'll see it for yourself soon enough," Big Ben suggested.

"Sit back? This is too thrilling. I can't just sit back!" Roscoe jogged over to the side of the trailer and looked up the tall, slick wall. He reached up with his front paws, but they slid against the smooth metal. He tried to find a foothold, but his back paws were just as worthless. "This is like running in place," Roscoe complained, panting. "How's a mouse supposed to see the sights if he's stuck on the floor?" He wiped his brow and sighed.

Happy sighed, too. "All right, Roscoe," he said, giving his friend a small smile. "This won't hurt a bit." Happy lowered his head and closed his teeth gently on the mouse's tail. When Happy lifted his head, Roscoe dangled in the air.

"Whoa! What if I were afraid of heights?" Roscoe yelled, swinging in the air. As Happy pushed his nose toward the window, Roscoe grasped at the sill with his front paws.

"But I know that you're not afraid of heights," Happy said, after opening his mouth and letting the mouse's tail go. "Besides, you're safe with me. And now you can see!"

"You're right." Roscoe leaned back against the window frame and put his paws behind his head. "Thanks," he added, looking out the window at the trees whizzing by. The rush of air pushed the mouse's whiskers back against

his cheeks. Roscoe laughed, curving his paw so it swerved up and down in the wind.

"Okay, you two," Goldi said, looking at Happy and Sassy. "We need to go over the rules before we get to town."

"Rules?" Happy asked. He glanced at Sassy. She looked surprised as well.

"Yes," Big Ben chimed in. "The town is a busy place. And it is very crowded for the parade. We need to stick together. And, as horses and ponies, we have to be careful. We don't want to step on anyone."

Happy looked up at the show horse. Big Ben's chestnut coat gleamed. He had a strong, rounded jawbone that made him look noble. Most of all, Happy was impressed with Big Ben's deep, brown eyes. They were wise with age and experience.

Happy listened carefully. He had never heard Big Ben sound so serious. He had thought the parade was going to be fun, but Big Ben's tone was making him nervous!

"Not everyone at the parade will be used to being around horses. Some people might even be afraid of you." Big Ben paused before continuing. "You need to listen closely to Andrea and Ivy. They will tell you what to do."

Happy and Sassy nodded. Roscoe stared out the window some more.

"Also," Goldi advised, "remember to stay calm. Don't let all the sights and sounds get to you."

Happy and Sassy nodded again. Goldi was shorter than the young ponies, but they still respected her. She was clever, and she knew a lot about working with people.

"So, do you understand the rules?" Big Ben asked.

Happy and Sassy took deep breaths, then each gave a final nod.

All of a sudden, Roscoe leaped up so he was standing on the windowsill. "We're here!" he yelled, pointing toward the town square. There was a lush, green lawn surrounded by shops and other buildings. "See the balloons and the banner? We're here! It's Spring Fling time!"

Chapter Five

Fair on the Square

"Wait! We're going past it!" Roscoe cried in alarm. The mouse watched the town square go by, his paw still pointing out the window. "Why didn't Diane stop?" he pouted.

"Not to worry," Big Ben said calmly. "There isn't room for all the trucks and trailers in the middle of town. Diane will park, and then we'll walk back to the parade grounds together."

Roscoe raised his eyebrows and nodded his head. He could contain his excitement a little longer.

Soon enough, the truck and trailer had come to a stop, and the Marshall family was busy unloading Big Ben and the ponies.

Ivy led Happy to a grassy plot next to a maple tree. "Did you have a good ride, boy?" she asked, before returning to the trailer to get his saddle. Happy threw his head in the air as a response, forgetting that Roscoe was perched between his ears.

"Whoa! Watch it, will you?" Roscoe scolded the brown pony. "Maybe you should put me down on the ground. It would probably be better if I explored town on my own."

"No!" Happy insisted. Roscoe running around the festival by himself? Happy could not think of a worse idea. "Stay right where you are, Roscoe. Remember what Big Ben said? One of the rules is that we have to stick together."

Roscoe rolled his eyes and waved off Happy's comment. "Those rules were for you and Sassy, not for me," said the mouse. "But I'll stay put if you stop throwing your head around all willy-nilly."

"Willy-nilly?" Happy asked with a little laugh.

"You know what I mean," Roscoe insisted. "Don't forget that I'm here."

Happy gave his head a slight nod. "It's a deal. I won't forget."

Before long, everyone was ready to walk to the town square. Big Ben and the ponies all wore saddles and bridles. Ivy rode Happy, and Andrea rode Sassy. Their father led Goldi — he planned to offer kids short rides along the parade route. Diane led Big Ben at the back of the group.

Happy wondered if Ivy had noticed Roscoe yet. Ivy knew that the mouse and pony were friends, but she had not said anything about the extra rider sitting between Happy's ears. There was so much to see! Happy understood if she missed the little mouse.

The walk to the town square did not take long. The trees on either side of the street grew tall and wide, creating a green canopy of leaves. The air was heavy with the smell of the lilies that sprang up in patches along the narrow road. It was still early in the morning, and the town seemed peaceful.

But as soon as the group neared the square, it was clear that the day was in full swing. Musicians on the bandstand blared ragtime music on their shiny brass instruments. Balloons bobbed from every old-fashioned streetlamp. There were people watering potted plants blooming with flowers of every color along the sidewalks. Other people unloaded trucks full of food carts and game booths. In the middle of the square, along the parade route, was a big Ferris wheel. Painted red with yellow seats and blue lights, it was the most amazing thing Happy had ever seen!

"Look, look, look!" chanted Roscoe. "It's beautiful. I wish we had one of those at Big Apple Barn. I would ride it all day long."

A man wearing a red-and-white-striped jacket motioned to Diane. He carried a clipboard and a pen. As he approached, he almost tripped over a basset hound. "And your name is?" he asked Diane, out of breath.

"We're from Big Apple Barn," Diane answered. "We're the Marshall family."

"Ah, yes," he replied, marking his list with a big check. "I'm Drake Dillon, the director of the festival." He looked at each of the Marshalls in turn. "The parade will start promptly at eleven o'clock, from the far corner of the square. You and your animals should line up under that first banner." The man pointed with his clipboard.

Happy looked up and saw a banner stretched between two streetlamps. It was white with green letters that read, THE SPRING FLING FESTIVAL.

"The parade route is marked by garlands," Drake continued. Again, he pointed with his clipboard, this time at the strands of flowers laced along the sides of the street. Ivy, Andrea, and their parents nodded at Drake.

"You will hear a bugle mark the start of the parade. I'll be at the bandstand, away from this zoo." Drake shook his hand at all the animals nearby, and then blushed. "Let me know if you need anything," he sputtered, before turning to a woman who was pulling a wagon full of Dalmatian puppies wearing fireman helmets.

Next to the woman was a girl riding a horse. "Hello, Happy," the horse said.

Happy was surprised to hear his name, but then he recognized the horse. She was very stylish, with a dark brown coat and a long, black mane and tail. He had met her at a show the year before.

"You know her?" Roscoe asked in Happy's ear. Happy nodded.

"Hello, Dazzle Me," replied Happy. "You're here for the parade?"

"I don't really care about the parade," the horse said. "We're here for the costume contest. Whoever wins gets to be the mascot of the festival! I think it should be me."

Happy looked at the horse and realized that she had big bows tied in her mane, and she wore a long pink blanket with tassels hanging from it. A sash was tied around her neck. It said, SPRING FLING QUEEN.

"Your blanket is lovely," Sassy spoke up.

Happy quickly introduced the horse to Sassy. "You both go to lots of shows," he said. "You'll probably see each other at one." Happy remembered how much Dazzle Me liked shows. She also seemed to like winning.

"Well, you two don't have very good costumes," the horse commented. "I don't think you can win Spring Fling mascot with just a saddle and bridle, but good luck." With that, Dazzle Me followed her owner away.

Chapter Six

Sticking Together

"I didn't know about the contest!" Sassy exclaimed. "Why aren't we dressed up? I could have been Spring Fling Queen if I had known."

"Yeah," Roscoe said. "Who does that horse think she is?" The mouse stamped his foot down on Happy's head.

Happy could hardly feel it. He didn't mind much about the contest. He was just thrilled to be at the parade! But Sassy liked to go

44

to shows and compete. Happy wasn't surprised that she wanted to be part of the contest.

"Dazzle Me's saddle blanket was pretty, but it wasn't very springy. I could have come up with something better, something with flowers and real pizzazz." Sassy's silky black ears pointed back as she spoke.

Happy gave Sassy a long look. After all, they didn't get to decide whether to be in the contest or not. It was up to Andrea and Ivy. Happy was glad that Ivy didn't make a big fuss about shows and ribbons and costumes.

Just then, Diane spoke up. "Okay, everyone," she said. "We have some time before the parade. Let's look around! Ivy and Andrea, how about you lead Sassy and Happy for now. You can ride them when the parade starts."

Happy looked at his surroundings again. A lot more animals and owners had arrived for the parade. There were cats, dogs, birds, and many other ponies and horses.

"Hey! Check it out. That pig is wearing a superhero cape!" Roscoe yelled. "And that dog has pink toenails. Hilarious!"

Happy had never seen anything like it. He was not as interested in the animals as the town itself. The square wasn't as big as the pasture at Big Apple Barn, yet the grass was just as green. There were buildings on all four sides — two sides were shops and the other two were houses. All of the buildings looked old, but the owners took good care of them.

Happy was careful as Ivy led him around. He tried to listen closely to what she asked him to do. He took small steps, but he still bumped into people walking in the other direction.

In the meantime, Roscoe couldn't stop chattering. He wanted to go everywhere — even to the florist and the yarn store.

"Hey! Get Ivy to take us into The Sweet Shoppe! Or the ice-cream parlor — over a hundred flavors! It looks like they make the ice cream right there. Let's go," Roscoe begged. "Or we could ride the Ferris wheel. It would be better at night, with the lights on and everything. But I'd go on it now. Maybe I could go more than once!"

Happy paused, making sure Roscoe was not going to launch into another round of requests. "Roscoe, if you haven't figured it out, I am a pony," Happy said. "I can't just walk into a candy store or fit on the Ferris wheel."

Since Roscoe was sitting between his ears, Happy couldn't see him — but he could hear the mouse's sigh. "I kind of forgot," Roscoe explained. "It's okay for now. I don't mind just looking." He sat down and nestled into Happy's mane.

"But you know," the mouse said, "you aren't as tall as some of the horses. And these booths are in the way. I can't see everything! I bet I could get a better view from over there, at the bandstand." Roscoe tugged on Happy's ear, so the pony knew where he was pointing.

"Roscoe," Happy said, "I can't take you over there unless Ivy wants to go that way. And I think Big Ben was right. We really should stick together!"

But at that moment, someone carrying a giant bouquet of cotton candy walked by Happy. There were at least twenty bags of the yummy treat in different colors, all attached to a large pole. The vendor carried them up over his head. Hanging there, the cotton candy bags looked like a giant, colorful cloud.

Happy hardly noticed as his head brushed against one of the bags.

Roscoe glanced up too late, and the candy knocked the mouse over. He closed his eyes, certain he would plunge to the ground. But at the last minute, he reached out. His tiny claws grasped the cotton candy bag. He held on tight!

Chapter Seven

Roscoe's Rampage

"Happy! Happy! Help!" Roscoe yelled, but the excitement of the growing crowd muffled his cries. Roscoe clung to the cotton candy bag. He gulped. It felt like he was slipping. He looked up to see that the bag was ripping! His sharp claws were tearing the bag in two.

"Oh!" Roscoe yelped. He grabbed at the bag with his other paw and dragged himself up, gasping and pulling. Before Roscoe realized it, he had crawled through the hole: He was *inside* the bag, sitting on top of a pink mountain of cotton candy.

"This is kind of cozy," the mouse said out loud. "And the view is good. Might as well rest a bit." He nestled into the squishy stuff until he was comfortable.

The vendor was walking all around the festival, weaving in and out of the game booths and the lines for rides. At first, Roscoe watched wide-eyed, taking in everything that went by. But before too long, he found he was sinking lower and lower in the fluffy pink haze. Roscoe tried to pull himself up, but he couldn't move his front or back legs. He was stuck in the sticky cotton candy!

"What do I do? What do I do?" the mouse murmured to himself. But he knew there was only one thing he could do. He had to eat his way out.

Roscoe took a big bite, and the cotton candy melted in his mouth. The next bite did the same. "This isn't so bad," Roscoe said with relief. "This will be easy." Just as he was able to move his front paws, he felt a quake. The whole bunch of bags shook as the vendor lowered the pole.

"What color do you want?" the vendor asked a little boy.

"Pink," the boy replied with an eager smile.

Roscoe gasped as he realized what was happening. He saw a hand reach for his bag of cotton candy! Roscoe shook his back legs free and ran. He scurried right over the vendor's hand and leaped to the ground.

"What? Wait! Where'd he come from?" Roscoe heard the vendor yell. The mouse didn't dare look back, but he couldn't run very fast. The cotton candy was still in his fur and between his toes. He felt sticky all over!

He tripped, and dirt clung to the hair on his tummy. Roscoe hid behind a hot-dog cart, panting. His fur was matted with dirt, and the lingering smell of cotton candy was making him light-headed. He crawled underneath the cart to catch his breath. He needed a plan.

Then Roscoe heard the gentle splash of water and thought about how much he could use a bath. Even his whiskers were a mess. What he wouldn't give for a Big Apple Barn water bucket right about now! It was his favorite way to rinse off at the stables.

Roscoe put his hand up to his ear. The little mouse followed the playful *splash-splash* over to one of the game booths.

"Step right up and try your luck!" the booth owner called. "If you can toss a quarter onto a floating boat, you win a prize. It's easy as pie."

Roscoe looked up. He didn't want to throw a quarter. He just wanted to take a dip. He nibbled on the end of his tail, which he always did when he was nervous. He was a small mouse, wasn't he? He could dive in without anyone noticing and slip back out again, couldn't he?

Roscoe decided to try his luck. He crawled up the back side of the booth. Sure enough, once he reached the top, there was a shallow pool of water, filled with mouse-sized plastic boats. Roscoe dipped his toes in the water. *Oooh!* It was cold. He looked over at the crowd. No one was waiting to play the game. Now was as good a time as any.

He did a cannonball into the tub, immediately rubbing his fur to get rid of the gooey clumps of sugar and dirt. But the water was so cold, Roscoe found it hard to breathe. He doggy-paddled over to a boat. Climbing inside, he shivered.

As the boat neared the edge of the tub, Roscoe realized it was the perfect chance to get out of the water without anyone seeing him. Just as his soggy arm reached for the side, a broad-shouldered teenager stepped up to the booth.

"I'll play your game," he said to the owner. "It better not be a scam." The teen cracked his knuckles and fished a quarter from his pocket.

Roscoe ducked down in the boat. He'd have to wait. He would crouch in the tiny blue tugboat in the corner and hope no one noticed him.

"Three tries," the owner announced.

Roscoe watched as the first quarter bounced off a miniature sailboat onto the grass. The second hit the water and sunk to the bottom. The third quarter headed straight for the little tugboat in the corner — and Roscoe's head!

"A mouse!" yelled the boy, pointing. In his attempt to get away, the boy tripped over the corner of the booth. The water in the pool spilled out in a giant wave.

Roscoe struggled to keep his head up as the wave sloshed onto the ground. The rush of water drowned out the squeals and screams of the crowd. Roscoe didn't even see the booth owner's face turn bright red as he shook his fist. Once the little mouse landed, he gave himself a quick shake, knocked the water from his ears, and ran. He was too fast to notice the cotton-candy vendor and booth owner chasing him.

After a few minutes, he took a break. In the distance, Roscoe could see the bandstand. It looked like the man in the red-and-white jacket was onstage. Roscoe knew that Drake Dillon was about to announce the start of the parade. If Roscoe could find his way to the bandstand, maybe he could get Happy's attention. He needed to get back to his friend!

With new hope, Roscoe set off toward the stage. The festival grounds were like a maze. As he passed people and booths and tables and rides, Roscoe felt like he was walking in circles.

But then he noticed something new. A smell. It wasn't honeysuckle. It wasn't lilies. It wasn't cotton candy. In fact, it wasn't sweet at all. He took another whiff. It was the most delicious scent that had ever reached Roscoe's nose.

"Oh, my!" exclaimed Roscoe.

The mouse hesitated. He needed to find Happy, but something told him he needed to follow that smell, too. After all, today was about adventure. Roscoe was not going to let a chance like this pass him by!

With his nose as a guide, Roscoe stumbled into a corner of the fairgrounds. The section was roped off. In the center was a table with a long white cloth draped over it.

Roscoe sniffed again. The smell was stronger here, and it came from on top of the table. "It won't be long now," he whispered.

Several people stood nearby, talking. Many of them wore aprons. One woman held a bright blue ribbon in her hands.

Hmmph. Why aren't they eating? Roscoe thought, with a shake of his head. *Who could*

59

resist that delicious smell? I don't think I'll ever understand people.

Roscoe tiptoed right by the group. He grabbed ahold of the tablecloth and pulled himself up. As he neared the top, he caught a glimpse of the most magnificent sight in the world. Cheese!

Roscoe's mouth watered as he heaved his hind legs onto the table. He scampered to

the smelliest hunk of cheese, the one with a blue ribbon on it.

"Hooray!" he squeaked before biting off more than he could chew.

Just then, the cheese makers turned toward the table.

"Mouse!" they yelled.

Chapter Eight

A Mouse Is Missing

Happy had no idea how long Roscoe had been gone. In fact, he didn't realize Roscoe was missing at all! The pony had been busy following Ivy around the town square, taking in all the sights. He thought Roscoe had finally grown tired of begging Happy to stop at booths, or asking Happy to wait so he could take a whirl on the bumper-car ride. Happy was relieved that Roscoe was no longer calling out to him every other minute.

But when Ivy led him up to the big, circular ride where beautiful painted horses rose up and down with the music, Happy had to get Roscoe's opinion.

"Hey, Roscoe," Happy whispered. "Ivy said this thing is called a merry-go-round. It doesn't look all that merry to me. Those horses are just going in circles!"

At first when Roscoe did not reply, Happy thought the mouse was giving him the silent treatment. Happy knew Roscoe might have been upset with him for not stopping at the waffle stand. But then another minute passed, and there was still no squeak from his big-eared buddy. That's when Happy realized Roscoe wasn't on top of his head anymore!

"Sassy! Sassy!" Happy called. The other pony looked back from where she was standing with Andrea. "Have you seen Roscoe?" he asked. When the appaloosa shook her head, Happy knew that Roscoe was missing.

Happy wished he had some way of telling Ivy. He wasn't even sure that Ivy realized the mouse had come with them in the first place. Roscoe had been sitting on Happy's head for most of the morning, but he had a way of huddling close to Happy's ears, so it was easy not to notice him. If Ivy found out about Roscoe's disappearance, Happy knew she'd help search the whole town square. Roscoe could be anywhere! What if he went to the candy store, or got trapped in the freezer at the ice-cream parlor?

"Time to head over to the start of the parade," Diane called from the front of their group. "Andrea, Ivy, how about you go ahead and get in the saddle?"

Happy was relieved to have Ivy on his back again. It would be easier to stay on the lookout for Roscoe if he did not also have to keep an eye on where Ivy was going.

As the sisters climbed onto the ponies, Happy told Sassy that Roscoe had vanished. Sassy passed the news on to Goldi, who then shared it with Big Ben. Happy could see the concern in everyone's eyes.

"The town is no place for a mouse to be lost," said Big Ben.

"Especially during the Spring Fling," agreed Goldi.

"I know, I know," answered Happy. He felt awful. How long had Roscoe been gone?

"Here's what we'll do," Sassy said, swishing her tail. "Big Ben and Goldi will watch that side. We'll look over here, Happy."

"That's good." Big Ben said. "The parade will take us around the entire festival. We'll find our mouse."

The horse and ponies kept watch, hoping to see a tiny gray mouse skitter across the street. But it was hard for them to see their own hooves. There were people and animals everywhere!

Before long, the Marshalls, Big Ben, and the ponies had arrived under the giant festival banner. They lined up behind an old-fashioned convertible with its top down. There was a man with wire-rimmed glasses and a driving scarf at the wheel, and a long-haired cat with bright blue eyes sitting on a velvet cushion in the backseat. A tiny, jeweled tiara rested on her head. A girl and a boy sat on either side of her.

When a bugle sounded, the parade

officially began. The brass band belted out a cheery tune from the stage, and Happy marched in time. But he was not enjoying the parade as much as he had thought he would. He was too worried about Roscoe!

There were clowns on stilts, and jesters juggling on unicycles. There were animals everywhere, but no mouse. People lined the street, clapping and pointing at the best costumes for the mascot contest.

Where is Roscoe? Happy thought. *He'd love this.*

Happy looked up as he heard a harsh, crackling sound. It was a microphone. The man in the red-and-white jacket, Drake Dillon, was standing in the center of the bandstand again, ready to speak.

"Welcome, one and all, to the Annual Spring Fling and Pet Parade," Drake said into the microphone. "It's with great pleasure that —"

Drake's voice suddenly cut off. Everyone stopped along the parade route to see what had happened. The festival director had a scowl on his face as he tapped the top of the

microphone with his fingers. Happy could see his lips move, but could not hear what he was saying.

Big Ben and the ponies stopped and stared. Something was going on!

Drake threw his hands up in the air and looked around. He finally pulled at the microphone cord.

"Ahhhhhhh!" The man's yell boomed over the parade grounds. The entire brass band was pointing and laughing at something on the bandstand floor. "A mouse!" Drake bellowed. "A mouse bit through the microphone wires!"

Chapter Nine

The Runaway Rodent

"Get that mouse!" the festival director cried, pointing down and leaping all around the stage. "He chewed through the sound system wires!"

A group of people rushed toward the bandstand.

"That mouse ruined my cotton candy!" roared the vendor.

"That mouse knocked over my boat game!" shouted the booth owner.

"That mouse ate my prizewinning cheese!" shrieked a woman wearing an apron.

"Get him!" they all hollered at once.

Happy struggled to figure out what was happening, but he wasn't tall enough to see the floor of the stage. *Get out of there!* Happy thought, hoping that Roscoe had the good sense to run.

Everyone was darting in different directions. Happy thought he could make out the vendor, the booth owner, and the cheese maker zigzagging across the square, their arms stretched out in front of them. Other people were running in the opposite direction, scanning the ground and yelping at any passing shadow.

"What's the big deal?" Happy asked, turning to Sassy.

The appaloosa cocked her head to the

side. "I don't know," she responded. "I guess some people don't like mice."

The ponies' ears pricked forward as they heard the bugle sound again. "Proceed, proceed!" yelled Drake from the bandstand, motioning for everyone to move forward. "The parade must go on!"

Slowly, the clowns, cars, pets, and ponies started to move again. But even the people in the parade kept turning their heads. They

wanted to catch a glimpse of the runaway mouse.

"There he is!" Happy heard someone cry. By now, the crowd of people chasing Roscoe had grown. Happy winced as he imagined the mouse dodging feet and hands as he raced around the festival. From the yells of the crowd, Happy guessed Roscoe was still somewhere in the square.

"Where is he? I can't see him!" Sassy said.

"I don't know," answered Happy, still searching.

Then, out of the corner of his eye, Happy saw something move with a flash of speed. It was Roscoe!

Happy saw him grab a string. It was attached to a balloon. Suddenly, the mouse was floating in the air.

"There!" yelled Happy, motioning toward Roscoe with his nose.

Happy wasn't the only one who had spotted him. People were pointing up as Roscoe rose higher and higher. Then, all at once, he let go of the string.

"Oh, no!" Goldi cried.

But Roscoe had fallen right onto the Ferris wheel.

The ponies all gave nods of approval. "Smooth move," Big Ben murmured.

The vendor, booth owner, and cheese maker stood at the foot of the ride, all shaking their fists at the mouse. They yelled at the ride operator to stop the wheel and let them on. A crowd gathered around them, and the people on the ride began to point and exclaim as Roscoe inched out onto one of the wheel's spokes.

The ride was still spinning, and Roscoe rose higher in the sky. Now the mouse was almost directly over the parade route. He shielded his eyes from the sun, surveying the area. All at once, he started jumping up and down, and pointed right at Happy. Roscoe cupped his paws around his mouth and shouted something to his friend.

Happy pricked his ears forward, but he could not understand what Roscoe was saying. The mouse gestured to the ground. Happy realized that the wheel was now headed down, and as soon as Roscoe was low enough, he would have to run from the crowd again.

Then Roscoe gestured once more, this time out toward the parade. Happy shook his head. "I don't understand," he whispered. Roscoe pointed again at the crowd below, then shrugged his shoulders.

The next thing Happy knew, Roscoe was scampering along the arm of the Ferris wheel, heading out toward the very tip. The mouse's legs moved faster and faster. Happy held his breath as Roscoe neared the end. Then, with a frantic leap, the mouse soared through the air.

Happy gulped. The mouse started to fall

faster and faster. Just as Happy was about to close his eyes, Roscoe grabbed hold of the flower garland that hung over the parade route. He dangled from it by one hand, and the flowers bobbed up and down.

"Wahoo!" Roscoe yelled.

Happy smiled at Sassy. They let out sighs of relief . . . just before the string of blooms broke in two. Like he was on a rope swing, Roscoe whooshed threw the air, heading

straight for the old-fashioned convertible. The driver ducked just in time. Roscoe's back paws knocked the tiara right off the cat's head! The mouse just kept swinging.

Happy watched as Roscoe zoomed toward him. "I love this place!" the mouse yelled in his ear as he flew by on the garland. Happy turned to see Roscoe let go of the flowery swing, land with a plop on the sidewalk, and dart out of sight.

Chapter Ten

A Fond Farewell

After Roscoe let go, the strand of flowers from his swing fell over Happy's shoulders. Happy hardly noticed as Ivy wrapped the blossoms around his neck. Then Ivy gently wove a few loose blooms in Happy's mane and tucked one under his bridle strap.

Ivy grinned at him. "That was one adventurous mouse! He reminded me of your friend, back at Big Apple Barn." She raised her eyebrows knowingly.

Happy's ear twitched, but he wasn't really listening. He was too shocked by what he'd just seen. Roscoe could have grabbed hold of Happy's bridle as he flew past, but he didn't. If he had, he would have been safe and sound with his friends. Happy wondered where the mouse was now.

Deep in thought, Happy plodded along the street. People pointed and remarked on the wreath of flowers that he wore around his neck. The petals were red, orange, and yellow. They were bright against the pony's brown coat and black mane. Happy could not have looked more festive if Ivy had spent hours planning a costume.

Before too long, Big Ben, Goldi, Sassy, and Happy had all walked under another Spring Fling banner, this one marking the end of the parade. Happy could not believe it was already over!

As Ivy slipped out of the saddle, Drake Dillon rushed to her side. "What's your pony's name, miss?"

"It's Happy," Ivy answered.

"Well, I must say, I love Happy's costume. The flowers are beautiful — sophisticated, but still simple. It's just the way we like to think of our little festival." He paused and looked around, his chin raised. "Everyone, I'd like to announce that Happy is our Spring Fling mascot!"

The crowd burst into applause. Drake Dillon smiled, pleased with his selection. He gave Happy an awkward pat.

"But he's not wearing a costume," Ivy tried to explain.

"No excuses, young lady. Happy's our winner," Drake insisted. "Now smile for the camera!"

*   *   *

Later that afternoon, Happy grazed alongside the trailer with his friends while the Marshalls enjoyed the rest of the festival.

Happy took a last bite of grass before raising his head. "Now's as good a time as any," he said to Sassy. The appaloosa gave a quick snort of agreement.

The two ponies tugged their lead lines with their teeth, easing the knots loose. They knew it wasn't right, but they did not intend to run away.

"We'll be back soon," Happy called in Big Ben's and Goldi's direction.

The noble horse nodded, and Goldi gave a soft nicker. Happy was certain they understood. He and Sassy had to rescue Roscoe!

The ponies paused by the trailer to discuss their plan. "How will we find him?" Sassy

asked with a toss of her mane. "He could be anywhere. Remember how he wanted to go to the ice-cream parlor and the hot-dog stand? Or maybe he found a hole into one of the little houses on the square. He could have already moved in there."

"I don't think so," Happy replied, shaking his head. Even though the mouse said he loved town, Happy knew his friend. "I think we should go this way." Happy tilted his head toward a tree-lined path.

"But that leads away from town," Sassy said.

"I know."

"Okay, then," Sassy replied. The two ponies started out, side by side. They didn't say anything more, just searched high and low for a tiny, gray mouse.

When they came to a clearing full of fresh, spring grass, Happy stopped. "This is it," he announced. He set off for a green patch spotted with sunlight.

"Hello, Roscoe," Happy said in greeting. He pushed his nose against the snoozing mouse.

Roscoe sat up and rubbed his eyes. "Hello, Happy. Hello, Sassy," the mouse said, nodding at each of the ponies. "How'd you find me?"

"Well, it wasn't that hard," Happy admitted. "I just thought about what you wanted to do today. You planned to chew on some wires, which you did. And eat a good snack, which you did. Then take a nap in the sun. And here you are."

"How'd you know I had a snack?" Roscoe asked, lifting his hands in question.

"I think the cheese maker chasing you all over the town square was a good hint," Sassy said.

"Oh, yeah. That was some good cheese," Roscoe admitted, pulling on one of his whiskers.

"So, since you've done everything you planned, how about we head home now?" Happy suggested.

"What if I want to stay?" Roscoe asked.

Happy and Sassy looked at each other, but didn't say a word.

"Oh, all right," Roscoe said. He stood up and brushed himself off. "Twist my tail. You know I could never leave Big Apple Barn. This town has good cheese, but it doesn't have my friends."

Happy lowered his head, and Roscoe scampered up his halter. He took a seat between Happy's ears.

The three friends strolled back to the trailer, where they waited with Goldi and Big Ben for the Marshalls to return.

As Ivy loaded Happy into the trailer, she offered him a carrot. "Here you go, boy. You were great today." Then she reached into her pocket and pulled out a square of cheese, which she placed in Roscoe's paws. "And so were you. I thought that was you, causing all that fuss! You sure made things exciting."

Roscoe bit into the cheese with his two front teeth and smiled.

"Now let's go home," Ivy said, petting Happy on the muzzle.

Diane lifted the ramp and closed the trailer door.

Before too long, Happy heard the truck engine sputter. The truck pulled the trailer along the small, tree-lined streets.

"M-mmm," Roscoe cleared his throat, and looked up at Happy. "May I?" he asked, pointing to the window. Happy rolled his eyes, but he could not say no to the little mouse. He bent his head down so that Roscoe could scramble onto the windowsill.

"Look!" Roscoe pointed at the town square as they drove past. "There it is! Good-bye, town," he called, waving his paw. "We had fun, but now we're going back to Big Apple Barn."

Happy glanced over at Big Ben, Goldi, and Sassy. They all let out sighs of relief. It would be good to be home. Roscoe had made the Spring Fling a festival to remember. And to think that the mouse had said that he didn't even want to go to the parade!

Roscoe was still waving at the town. The mouse leaned out the window to watch as the Ferris wheel, bandstand, and other attractions disappeared from sight. "Thanks for a fun day!" he called. "We'll see you again next year!"

"We wouldn't miss it!" Happy added.

Then Roscoe turned and winked at his friend. Happy winked right back.

Glossary
How a Horse Sees

In the wild, horses and ponies are animals of prey, which means that other animals hunt them for food. They rely on their sight to keep them safe.

Horses' eyes are on the sides of their heads, which allows them to see different things out of each eye. They can see almost every-thing that happens around them! Their only "blind spots" are directly in front of them (at the forehead and nose) and directly behind them (at their tail).

You should never approach a horse from behind, because they can't see you! While they can sense movement much better than a person, they cannot focus as easily as we can. You might scare them!

About the Author

Kristin Earhart grew up in Worthington, Ohio, where she spent countless waking and sleeping hours dreaming about horses and ponies. She started riding lessons at eight, and her trainer really was named Diane. Kristin's pony, Moochie, and her horse, Wendy, were two of the best friends a girl could have. She lives in Brooklyn, New York, with her husband and their son.